Vitaly Bianki

Forest Homes

DRAWINGS BY MAI MITURICH

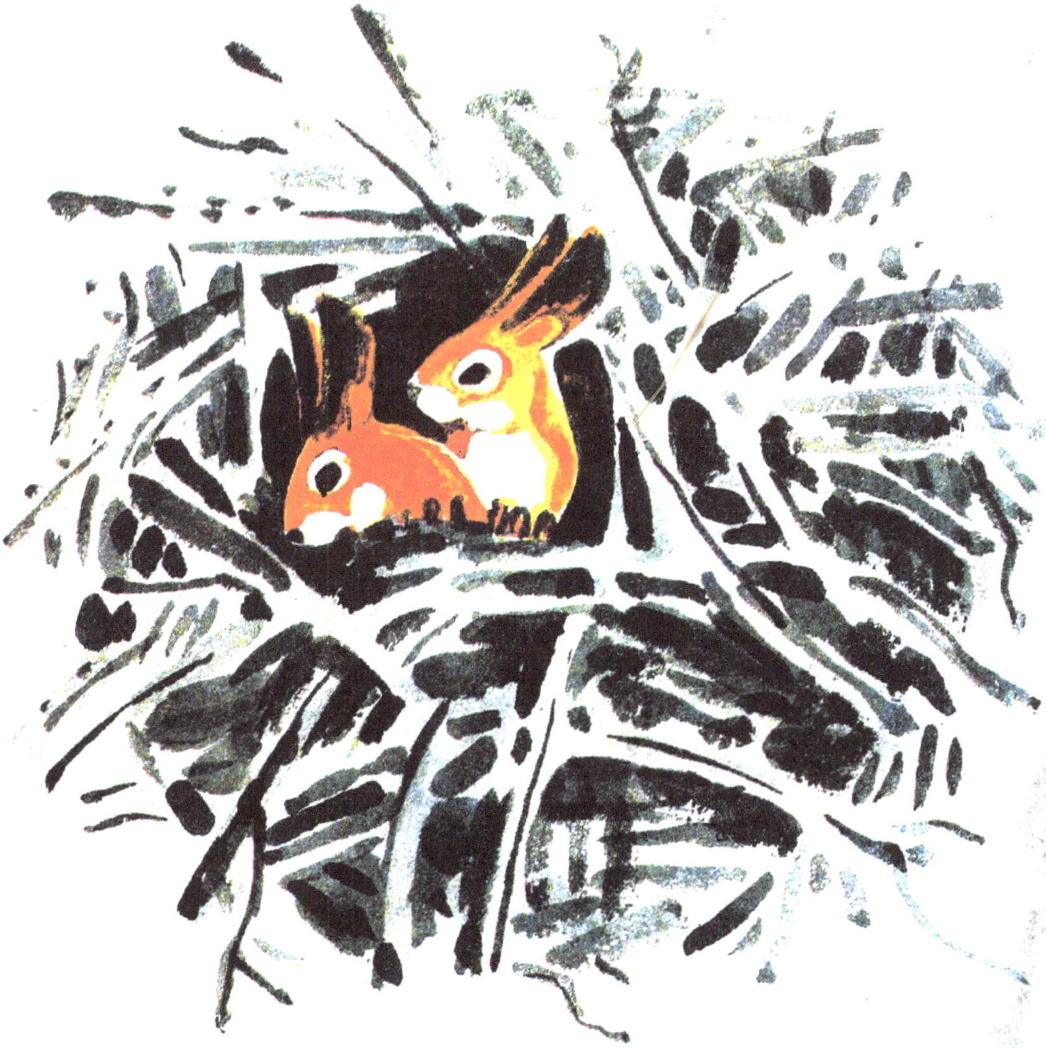

INSIGHT PUBLICA ®

INSIGHT PUBLICA ®

Nadakkave, Kozhikode, Kerala
Tel:0495–4020666
www.insightpublica.com
e-mail: insightpublica@gmail.com

Forest Homes

Vitaly Bianki

Illustrated by Mai Miturich
Translated by Irina Zheleznova
First Published by Raduga Publishers, Moscow USSR
Insight Publica facsimile edition: June 2020
Copyright©Reserved

ISBN 978-93-89804-67-6

Published by
Insightinpublica Publishers Pvt. Ltd.
Printed at Repro India Limited, India

Those fantastic
Soviet Books Again

All of us still have those fond memories of the books from the erst-while Soviet Union, which were once extensively circuated here, in Kerala - books of fabulous tales, riveting scientific facts and enchanting illustrations which stole the readers' hearts. They left in us an indelible impression and an unforgettable reading experience. An experience still ever-green in us, Malayali diaspora.

As the Union got dissolved, those charming books of tales too vanished, turning them into cherished memories of nostalgia. Yet, readers have relentlessly been looking for those inimitable books. That was why we, the INSIGHT PUBLICA, published a few of them in the same mode. We are grateful and glad to say that readers whole-heartedly backed us in realizing the project.

During the execution of our mission,we could fathom the depth and breadth of a great nation's remarkable literary project. Those sublime Soviet stories traversed in translation into many a nation and many a language. Those books were ubiquitous-not as merchandise, but as products of culture.

The fantastic bolstering that INSIGHT PUBLICA could get is the impetus that drove us daringly to undertake the mission of reprinting and republishing those Soviet works in Indian languages.

You readers need not anymore be discontented with the scanned copies of these books. INSIGHT PUBLICA will help reach into your hands those very books with the same freshness and warmth.

Let us present you again those fantastic Soviet Stories with humility and pride.

Sumesh Insight

В. Бианки

Лесные домишки

На английском языке

CONTENTS

FOREST HOMES 5
Translated by Fainna Glagoleva

RED HILL 18
Translated by Olga Shartse

ANT HURRIES HOME 32
Translated by Fainna Glagoleva

THE FIRST HUNT 43
Translated by Ronald Vroon

FOREST HOMES

High over the river, above a steep cliff, young river swallows darted back and forth chasing each other, shrilling and twittering. They were playing tag in the air.

Little Swallow was so quick that none of the other birds in the flock could catch her. She always managed to duck or dart away.

Whoever was "it" would chase after Little Swallow, and she would fly hither and thither, up and down, streaking off so fast her wings never stopped moving, not even for a moment.

Suddenly Falcon appeared in the blue sky. The wind whistled through the feathers of his sharply-curved wings.

The flock of swallows was terror-stricken. They scattered instantly, each swallow flying off in a different direction. In a flash they were gone.

Little Swallow never once looked back as she winged away

over the river, the wood and the lake beyond.

Falcon was a very dangerous bird to play tag with.

Little Swallow flew on and on until she had no strength to fly any farther. Then she turned to look back. No one was chasing her. She looked around and saw that she was in a strange place. She looked down and saw a river, but this was not a familiar river, it was one she had never seen before.

Little Swallow became frightened.

She could not recall the way back home and no wonder, for she had been so terrified she had never looked around to get her bearings.

It was late afternoon and would soon be evening. What was she to do?

She flew down, perched on a twig and wept bitterly. Suddenly, she saw a little yellow bird with a black neckband come running along the sand.

Little Swallow was happy to see it. "Won't you please tell me how to get home? " she said.

"Where are you from? "

"I don't know."

"You'll have a hard time finding your home if you don't know where it is. The sun will soon go down and then it'll be dark. Why don't you stay over at my house? My name is Plover, and I live nearby."

Plover ran off a few steps and pointed his beak at the sand. Then he bowed and swayed on his spindly legs and said, "Here's my house. Come on in."

Little Swallow looked hard, but could not see anything that resembled a house. All she could see were sand and pebbles.

"Can't you see it? Here, over here, where the eggs are."

Little Swallow finally made out the four speckled eggs lying among the pebbles right on the sand.

"What's the matter? Don't you like my house?"

Little Swallow didn't know what to say, for if she said it was no house at all, Plover would be hurt. That was why she said, "I'm not used to sleeping out in the open on cold sand that has nothing to cover it."

"That's too bad. Try Dove's house in the fir grove over there.

He has a house with a floor. You can spend the night there.''

"Thank you.'' Little Swallow flew off to the fir grove. She had no trouble finding Dove and asked him to let her spend the night at his house.

"All right, if you like it here.''

Actually, all there was to his house was a floor. It was as full of holes as a sieve. He had simply thrown some twigs across the branches every which way.

There were white eggs on the twigs. You could see them from below through the holes in the floor.

Little Swallow was surprised. "There's only a floor. Your house doesn't have any walls. How can you sleep here? ''

"Well, if you want a house that has walls, you'd better try Oriole's place. I think you'll like it.''

Dove told Little Swallow the address: the most beautiful birch tree in the grove.

Little Swallow flew off towards the birch grove. All the trees there seemed beautiful to her. She searched hard for Oriole's house until she saw a lovely little house attached to a small branch.

It seemed very cozy and looked just like a rose made of fine bits of gray paper.

"What a tiny house Oriole has! There's no room for me at all," Little Swallow said to herself. Still, she decided to knock. At that very moment a swarm of hornets came buzzing out of the little gray house. They swarmed around her and buzzed angrily. They looked as though they might sting her.

Little Swallow flew away from them as fast as she could, off through the bright-green leaves.

All of a sudden something gold and black flashed by. Then Little Swallow made out a golden bird with black wings on one of the branches.

"Where are you hurrying to, Little Swallow? "

"I'm looking for Oriole's house."

"I'm Oriole. My house is right here on this beautiful birch tree."

Little Swallow looked at the spot, but could not see anything except the green leaves and white branches of the tree. When she had a really good look she gasped.

There, high above the ground, a light, pocket-shaped basket

was attached to a little branch. It was beautifully woven of fibers, grass, strands of wool and hair, and bits of paper-thin birch bark.

"Oh! I'd never stay in such a flimsy house! It makes me dizzy just to see it swinging in the wind. It looks like it'll be blown away any minute. Besides, you have no roof."

Golden Oriole sounded hurt as she said, "Then go to Chiff-Chaff's house. If you're afraid of sleeping outdoors you'll probably like her tent, because it has a roof."

Little Swallow set off for Chiff-Chaff's house.

Yellow Chiff-Chaff lived in the grass near the birch tree where Oriole's hanging basket was.

Little Swallow liked her tent: it was made of dry grass and moss. "How cozy this is. It has a floor and walls, and a roof, and a feather bed. Just like our home."

Chiff-Chaff was very glad to have company. She was just telling Little Swallow where to sleep when the ground began to tremble. Little Swallow was frightened. She cocked her head and listened to the thundering noise, but Chiff-Chaff said:

"It's only some horses galloping towards the grove."
"Will your roof cave in if a horse steps on it? "
Chiff-Chaff nodded sadly.
"Oh, this is a terrible place! " Little Swallow darted out of the tent. "I'd never be able to sleep a wink here, what with worrying about being crushed to death. Our home is much safer. No one will ever step on you or dash you to the ground."
"You probably have a house like Grebe's," Chiff-Chaff said. "Her house isn't on a tree, so the wind can't blow it away, and it's

not on the ground, so no one can step on it. Do you want me to take you there? ”

“Yes! ”

And so they flew off to the lake to find Grebe.

There, on a little island of reeds surrounded by water was a large-headed bird. Its head feathers stuck up like tiny horns.

Chiff-Chaff said goodbye to Little Swallow and told her to ask the horned bird to let her stay for the night.

Little Swallow flew to the island in the middle of the lake. She was surprised to see it floating. It was a pile of dry reeds bobbing on the water. There was a dent in the middle of the pile and it was lined with soft swamp grass. Grebe’s eggs were on it, covered over with some thin dry reeds.

Grebe was perched on the edge of the floating island, sailing around the lake as if the island was a boat.

Little Swallow told Grebe about her search for a place to spend the night and asked if she could stay on the island.

“Are you afraid to sleep on the waves? ”

“But don’t you tie up at the bank for the night? ”

“My house isn’t a boat. It goes wherever the wind blows, so we’ll be rocking and bobbing all night.”

“I’m scared. I want to go home! ”

Grebe became angry. “My! Aren’t you fussy! Nothing seems

to please you!   Well, you go find yourself whatever you want."
And she chased Little Swallow away.

Little Swallow flew off. She was weeping bitterly, for it was
getting darker and darker. Soon she reached a dense wood and saw
a house on a large branch of a tall fir tree. It was round and made
of sticks and branches. The inside was lined with soft, warm moss.

"Just the place I've been looking for. It's sturdy and it has a
roof."

Little Swallow flew up to the big house, tapped on the wall

with her beak and said in a pitiful voice, "Won't you please let me in for the night?"

Suddenly a terrible brown furry head with bristling whiskers and yellow teeth appeared. The monster growled: "Since when do birds come knocking at squirrels' houses at night, asking to be let in?"

Little Swallow was frightened to death. Her blood froze. She darted away, soared over the wood and flew off as fast as she could, never once looking back.

She flew on and on until she had no strength to fly any

RED HILL

Chirp was a young red-headed sparrow. When he became a year old he married Chirpie and decided to set up house.

"But, darling, where can we build our nest? " Chirpie asked in their sparrow language. "All the tree hollows in our garden are occupied."

"Small matter! " Chirp replied cockily in the same sparrow language, of course. "We'll drive out our neighbours and take their hollow."

Chirp loved fighting and jumped at this chance to show Chirpie what a brave chap he was. And before his shy young wife could stop him, he rushed to the big mountain ash where the hollow was occupied by another young sparrow.

The owner was not at home, and Chirp said to himself: "I'll get into the hollow and when he comes back I'll start screaming that he's trying to seize my home. The old sparrows will come flying, and we'll give him what for! "

He had quite forgotten that his neighbour was married and that his wife had been working on their nest for five days.

Chirp poked his head into the hole, and got a painful peck on the nose. He sprang back. And there was the master of the house himself attacking him from behind. With loud cries they clashed in the air, fell on the ground, and rolled into the ditch.

Chirp was a great fighter, and his opponent was already weakening.

The noise brought the old sparrows from all over the garden. It did not take them long to tell right from wrong, and they gave Ghirp such a trouncing that he barely escaped from them with his life.

He came to in a clump of bushes where he had never been before. He ached all over.

Chirpie was sitting beside him, and the poor dear looked terribly frightened.

"Chirp, Chirp darling, we can never go back to our garden now! " She spoke so brokenly that Chirp would have surely burst into tears, if sparrows could cry. "Where are we going to hatch our young now? "

He knew very well that from now on he must keep out of the old sparrows' sight or they'd peck him to death. Still, he did not want Chirpie to see that he was afraid. And so he smoothed down his tousled feathers with his beak, pulled himself together, and said with his old carefree air:

"Small matter! We'll find ourselves another place, and a better one too! "

And they set off to look for a new place to live.

Just behind the bushes there was a jolly, blue river, and on the opposite side the bank rose in a very, very steep hill made of red clay and sand. Near the top of this hill there were lots of little holes and burrows. Magpies and windhovers sat in couples in front of the big holes, and swallows kept darting in and out of the smaller ones.

"Look, what fun they're having," Chirpie said, pointing to the flock of swallows racing this way and that. "Let's build our nest here too."

Chirp glanced nervously at the magpies and windhovers. "It's all right for the swallows, they dig their own nests in the sand. And what am I supposed to do? Start a fight to grab someone else's nest? " He ached all over again at the mere thought.

"No, I don't like it here," he said. "It's too noisy."

And they flew on.

Now they came to a grove, and beyond this grove they saw a cottage and a barn.

Chirp and Chirpie alighted on the roof of the barn, and the first thing Chirp noticed was that there were no swallows or sparrows about.

"Living will be fine here! " Chirp said happily. "See all those seeds and crumbs scattered all over the yard? We'll be by our-selves here, and we won't let anyone else in."

"Oh, Chirp, look at that horrible monster over there, on the porch! " Chirpie said in a terrified whisper.

The monster was Ginger, the fat Tom Cat, and true enough he was sleeping on the porch.

"Small matter! " Chirp said bravely. "What harm can he do us? Watch me give him one! "

He jumped off the roof and made straight for the monster, so recklessly that Chirpie cried out in alarm.

Taking the cat by surprise, Chirp very deftly snatched a bit of

dragged out the whole nest. In vain Chirpie screamed, in vain Chirp threw himself at the cat—no one came to their aid. The robber calmly ate all the six eggs. The wind easily lifted the empty nest and flung it down on the ground.

That same day, Chirp and Chirpie left the barn forever, and moved to the grove, out of the cat's reach.

Here they were lucky to find an empty tree hollow. Once again they started fetching bits of straw and feathers, and toiled for a whole weak, building a new nest.

Their nextdoor neighbours were Mr. and Mrs. Finch, Mr. and

Mrs. Flycatcher, and Mr. and Mrs. Goldfinch. Each couple had its own home, there was plenty of food for all, and still Chirp managed to pick a quarrel with them—for no reason really, simply because he loved a fight and wanted to show them how brave and strong he was.

The Finch, however, proved stronger than Chirp and taught him a good lesson. Chirp took care now: he no longer spoiled for a fight, and merely fluffed out his feathers and shouted something saucy when one of his neighbours flew past. This did not make them angry, because they themselves liked to boast of their strength and bravery in front of other birds.

The first to raise the alarm was the Finch. Although he lived farthest from the sparrows, Chirp heard his loud warning cry: Rium-pink-pink! Rium-pink-pink!

"Chirpie, come here quickly," he cried. "Hear the Finch's warning—there's danger! "

Indeed, someone frightening was creeping up on them. The Goldfinch now gave the alarm, and after him the Flycatcher. The enemy must be quite close if the Flycatcher could see him, because his home was only four trees away from Chirp's.

Chirpie flew out of the tree hollow and perched on the branch beside her husband. Their neighbours had warned them of the approaching danger, and they were prepared to face whatever was coming.

They caught the flicker of fluffy ginger fur in the bushes, and their mortal enemy—Tom Cat—stepped out into the clearing. Tom Cat saw that the sparrows had been warned by their neighbours,

and there was no catching Chirpie in her nest. He was very angry.

Suddenly the tip of his tail began to twitch in the grass, and his eyes narrowed into slits. Tom Cat must have seen their tree hollow. Six sparrow eggs for breakfast wasn't so bad, after all. He licked his lips, climbed up the tree, and reached into the hollow.

Chirp and Chirpie raised a scream for all the grove to hear. Again no one came to their aid. Their neighbours kept to their nests, screaming loudly from fear. Each couple was worried about the safety of its own home.

Tom Cat got his claws into the nest and pulled it out.

But this time he came too early: Chirpie had not laid any eggs yet.

Finding none, he threw the nest down in disgust, and slipped down to the ground. The sparrows screamed at him as he walked away.

He stopped when he came to the bushes, turned round and all but said:

"Just you wait, my pretty birds, just you wait! I'll get you

Chirp poked his head into the hole, and got a painful peck on the nose. He sprang back. And there was the master of the house himself attacking him from behind. With loud cries they clashed in the air, fell on the ground, and rolled into the ditch.

Chirp was a great fighter, and his opponent was already weakening.

The noise brought the old sparrows from all over the garden. It did not take them long to tell right from wrong, and they gave Ghirp such a trouncing that he barely escaped from them with his life.

He came to in a clump of bushes where he had never been before. He ached all over.

Chirpie was sitting beside him, and the poor dear looked terribly frightened.

Very soon they came to Red Hill.

"Come and stay with us! " the swallows called out to the sparrows in their own language. "Ours is a friendly, gay community! "

"That's what you say, but I bet you'll start a fight with us," Chirp said sulkily.

"Why should we fight? " the swallows replied. "There are enough midges here for everyone, and there are lots of empty holes here, on Red Hill, just take your pick! "

"And what about the windhovers? And the magpies? " Chirp went on.

"The windhovers feed on the grasshoppers and mice they catch out in the fields. They don't bother us. We're all good friends."

"We went everywhere, Chirp, but a nicer spot than this we never saw," said Chirpie. "Let's stay here."

"Oh well," Chirp said, giving in. "We might give it a try, seeing there are some empty holes and nobody's going to fight."

They flew close to the bank and, true enough, no one molested them—neither the windhovers, nor the magpies.

They went to have a look at the vacant holes, and found two to their liking—they were not too deep, and had a wide opening.

In one of them they built the nest, where Chirpie was to hatch her eggs, and in the other one, which was close beside it, Chirp was to sleep at night.

The swallows, magpies and windhovers had long hatched their eggs. Chirpie alone still brooded in her dark nest. Chirp was busy from morning till night bringing her nice things to eat.

A fortnight passed. Tom Cat did not show up, and the sparrows forgot all about him.

Chirp could not wait for the chicks to hatch. Every time he brought Chirpie a worm or a fly he asked:

"Not knocking yet? "

"No, not yet."

"Will they be much longer? "

"No, just a little longer," Chirpie replied patiently.

And then, one morning, Chirpie called to him from the nest:

"Come quickly! One has knocked! "

Chirp came flying. In one of the eggs the chick was knocking at the shell with his feeble little beak. The sound was faint, but he heard it.

Chirpie broke the shell in several places to help her chick.

It took him a few minutes to finish the job, and now he showed from the egg—a tiny, blind, plucked-looking chick, with a big head wobbling on a very, very thin neck.

"Isn't he funny! " Chirp exclaimed.

"He's not funny at all," Chirpie said touchily. "He's a very pretty chick. Make yourself useful and chuck those eggshells as far from the nest as you can."

By the time Chirp came back, a second chick had hatched, and one more had begun to knock.

It was at that precise moment that panic swept Red Hill.

From their nest the sparrows heard the shrill cries of the swallows.

Chirp jumped outside and returned at once with the awful news that Tom Cat was scrambling up the bank.

"He saw me! " Chirp cried. "He'll be here before we know it, and he'll get us together with the chicks. Be quick, let's fly away from here! "

"I'm not coming," Chirpie replied sadly. "I can't leave my chicks. Whatever will be, will be."

She remained deaf to Chirp's calls, and did not budge.

And then Chirp flew out of their hole and madly attacked the enemy. But Tom Cat still went on scrambling up the bank. The swallows circled angrily just overhead, the magpies and windhovers joined them, but Tom Cat quickly made the ledge and got a clutch at the sparrows' nesthole.

All he had to do now was thrust in his other front paw and pull out the nest together with Chirpie, the chicks and the eggs.

And here one of the windhovers pecked his tail and another gave him a hard peck on the head, while two of the magpies struck at his back.

Tom Cat spat from the pain, swung round to catch the birds with his front paws, but they ducked, and he went tumbling down. There was nothing for him to catch hold of. The sand rolled down together with him, faster and faster all the time.

The birds could not see him in the cloud of red dust rushing down the steep hill. Plop! When the dust had cleared away, they saw Tom Cat's wet head bobbing in the middle of the river, with Chirp hovering behind and pecking it.

Tom Cat swam to the opposite bank and climbed out. Chirp was on to him again, never leaving him alone. Tom Cat had had such a scare, that he did not dare make a grab at the sparrow, and, sticking out his wet tail, galloped home.

He was never seen on Red Hill again.

ANT HURRIES HOME

Ant climbed to the very top of the birch tree and looked down. He could barely make out his own anthill. He sat down on a leaf and said to himself, "I'll rest here for a while and then climb back down again."

The rules of an ant family are very strict: as soon as the sun begins to set all the ants must hurry home. When the sun does set they close all the tunnels and go to sleep. If an ant is late he has to spend the night outdoors.

The sun was dipping towards the forest, but Ant still sat there on the leaf. "I have plenty of time. It won't take long to run down," he said to himself.

The leaf he was sitting on was not a good leaf at all. It was yellow and dry. A sudden gust of wind tore it off the branch and carried it over the forest, over the river and away over the village.

Ant hung on to the leaf for dear life.

The wind carried it to a meadow beyond the village and there it fell, right onto a rock. The bump hurt Ant's legs.

"This is the end of me. I'll never get back home now. If my legs didn't hurt I'd get back home in no time, because this is all flat country, but they do and I can't. I could kick myself." This was what he was thinking as he lay on the ground.

Ant looked around and saw an inchworm. It was a worm like any other worm except that it had legs in front and legs in back.

"Inchworm, Inchworm, won't you take me home? All my legs ache," Ant said.

"You won't bite me, will you? "

"No."

"All right. Get on."

Ant climbed onto Inchworm's back. Inchworm curved his back and brought his rear legs forward. He set them down behind his front legs so that his tail was right behind his head. Then he suddenly raised his front legs off the ground and into the air till he was standing up straight. Then he flopped down, still as straight as a stick. He measured off his own height on the ground and arched his back again. And that is how he moved forward, measuring the ground all the way. Meanwhile, Ant was flying up and down, up

and down, legs up and head down over and over again.

"I can't take this any more! Stop, or I'll bite you! "

Inchworm stopped and stretched out on the ground. Ant jumped off. He could hardly catch his breath.

He looked around and saw a meadow covered with mown grass. Daddy-long-legs was walking along there. His legs were like stilts and his head bobbed up and down between them.

"Spider, Spider, won't you take me home? All my legs ache."

"All right, get on."

Ant had to climb up Spiders' leg as far as the knee, and then slide down his knee to his back, because a Daddy-long-legs' knees are higher than its back.

Spider began moving his stilts every which way, one here, the other there. His eight legs flashed up and down, making Ant's head spin. Spider was not moving fast at all, though. In fact, he was practically dragging his belly along the ground.

Ant soon got tired of this kind of a piggy-back ride. He was just getting ready to bite Spider when they reached a smooth, even path.

Spider stopped. "Get off. See that beetle? It's a scarab beetle, and it's much faster than I am."

Ant got off. "Beetle, Beetle, won't you take me home? All my legs ache."

"All right, get on. You can come along for the ride."

No sooner had Ant scrambled onto Beetle's back than they were off at top speed. Beetle's legs were as straight as a horse's. The six-legged steed galloped along as smoothly as if it were flying.

They soon reached a potato field.

"Get off. I can't manage these up-and-down rows. They're too steep for me. You'd better find another horse."

Ant had no choice. He had to get off.

As far as Ant was concerned, the potato vines might just as well have been a jungle. It would have taken him a whole day to

cross the field, even if his legs did not ache. The sun would soon be setting. Then Ant heard a squeak: "Come on, Ant, get on my back and we'll be off! "

Ant turned to see who it was. He saw a little flea. Flea was even smaller than he was.

"You'll never get me off the ground. See how small you are."

"You think you're so big? Come on, get on."

Ant finally managed to get himself seated on Flea's back, though his legs hung over the sides.

"All set? "

"I guess so."

"Hang on."

Flea tucked his strong hind legs under him. When they were folded up they were just like little springs. Click! And they opened up. Flea hopped to the top of a row. Click! They were on another row. Click. They were on a third row. And so they hopped along until they reached a fence.

"Can you hop over the fence? " Ant asked.

"No, it's too high. Ask Grasshopper. He can."

"Grasshopper, Grasshopper, won't you take me home? All my legs ache."

"Get on."

Ant got on Grasshopper's back.

Grasshopper folded his hind legs in half and then quickly straightened them out. This sent him high into the air, just as it had Flea. But then Grasshopper suddenly opened his wings with a great crackling sound and flew over the fence. They settled slowly to the ground on the other side.

"This is as far as I'm going. You'll have to get off here."

Ant saw a river ahead. He would never be able to swim across it.

The sun was much lower now.

"I can't jump across the river, either. It's too broad. But wait! I'll call Waterbug! He'll ferry you across," Grasshopper said. He made a sawing sound. Soon a little boat on legs came gliding across the water. When it got closer Ant saw it was not a boat at all. It was Waterbug.

"Waterbug, Waterbug, won't you take me home? All my legs ache."

"All right, get on."

As soon as Ant had got on Waterbug's back, he set off across the water, just as if he were walking on land.

By now the sun had nearly set.

"Can't you go any faster? Please try. They won't let me in if I'm late."

"I'll try," Waterbug said and scurried along as fast as he could, shoving hard with his hind legs and then sliding along as if he were skating on ice. They reached the other bank in no time.

"Can't you walk on land? "

"No. It's awfully hard, because my feet don't glide there. And anyway, there's a forest ahead. You'd better find yourself another horse."

Ant looked up. The trees in the forest reached high into the sky, and the sun had gone down behind the trees. Alas! He would never be home on time.

"There's a horse for you coming our way," Waterbug said.

Indeed, there was big clumsy Maybug. No, that sort of a horse would never do! Still, Ant took Waterbug's advice and said, "Maybug, Maybug, won't you take me home? All my legs ache."

"Where do you live? "

"In the anthill beyond the forest."

"That's a long way off. Well, all right! Get on."

Ant climbed up Maybug's hard side.

"All set? "

"Yes."

"Where are you? "

"On your back."

"Silly! Get on my head."

Ant climbed onto Maybug's head. It was a good thing he did, because a moment later Maybug's back split in two to make two hard wings that were just like two upside-down scoops.

No sooner had Maybug raised his hard wings than a pair of silky, transparent wings opened up from under them. The silky wings were longer and wider than the hard top wings.

"Huff, huff, huff! " went Maybug, puffing away as if he was starting up a motor.

"Can't you hurry, please? Please?"

Maybug did not reply. He just went on huffing. Then his transparent little underwings began to move. Faster and faster they went. Zzz! Zzz! Tuck-tuck-tuck! Maybug rose straight up into the air like a cork popping out of a bottle. Higher and higher he went over the treetops.

From this great height Ant saw the rim of the sun touching the earth. They were going so fast it took Ant's breath away. Zzz! Tuck-tuck-tuck! Maybug cut through the air like a bullet.

The forest flashed below and was gone. There was the familiar birch tree and the anthill at its foot. When they were right over the top of the birch the Maybug turned off his motor and plopped down on one of the branches.

"How will I get down? My legs still ache. I'll surely break my neck."

Maybug folded his silky wings and then covered them with his hard top wings, carefully tucking the edges of the silky wings under the hard scoops. He was silent for a moment and then said, "I don't know how you're going to get down. I know I'm not going to take you. You ants bite too hard. So you'd better manage as best as you can."

Ant looked down at his home under the tree. Then he looked at the sun. The earth had already swallowed half of it.

Ant looked around, but all he saw were leaves and branches, branches and leaves.

He would never reach home in time. And he couldn't dive down!

Suddenly he saw Caterpillar on a leaf close by, spinning a silken thread and winding it around a little twig.

"Caterpillar, Caterpillar, won't you help me get down? I just have a minute left. I'll have to spend the night outdoors if I'm late."

THE FIRST HUNT

Puppy was sick and tired of chasing chickens around the yard.

"I'm going to track down wild birds and beasts," he decided.

So he wriggled under the gate and ran toward the meadow.

As he ran about, wild beasts and birds and insects saw him. And each began to think to himself.

"I'm going to trick him! " thought Bittern Bird.

"I'll surprise him! " thought Hoopoe Bird.

"I'll give him a fright! " thought Wryneck Bird.

"I'll give him the slip! " thought Lizard.

The caterpillars, the butterflies, and the grasshoppers all thought: "We'll hide from him! "

"And I shall drive him away! " thought Bombardier Beetle.

"We can all stand up for ourselves, each in his own way! " they all thought to themselves.

Meanwhile Puppy had run up to the pond and spied Bittern, standing by the reeds on one leg. The water reached to her knee.

"O-ho! " thought Puppy, "I'll catch her right now." He poised himself to spring onto her back. But Bittern glanced at him and strode into the reeds.

The wind whipped about the pond. The reeds bent and swayed
back and forth
back and forth.
Brown and yellow stripes swayed before Puppy's eyes
back and forth
back and forth.
Bittern stood in the reeds, all painted in yellow and brown stripes. She stood and she swayed
back and forth
back and forth.

Puppy opened his eyes wide and stared and stared, but he could not spot Bittern in the reeds.

"Huh," he thought, "Bittern has tricked me. I'm not about to jump into an empty patch of reeds! I'll just catch myself another kind of bird."

He ran over to a hillock and gazed about. There sitting on the ground was Hoopoe. The bird was playing with his topknot, now opening it wide, now closing it tight.

"Aha! " thought Puppy, "I'll pounce on him from this hillock right now! "

But Hoopoe fell to the ground, spread his wings, opened his

tail, and raised his beak in the air.

Puppy stared. There was no bird at all, only a many-coloured rag from which a crooked needle protruded.

Puppy marvelled. What had become of Hoopoe?

"Could I really have taken this coloured rag for a bird?

I'll hurry off and catch a small bird! "

He dashed over to a tree and sure enough a small bird was perched on one of its branches, Wryneck.

Puppy rushed at her, but Wryneck scuttled into a hollow in the tree.

"Oho! " thought Puppy. "I have her now! " He stood up on

through the air flew butterflies.

Puppy took off after them, but all of a sudden everything about him changed. It was like a special picture: all were right there, but he couldn't see them. Everyone was hiding.

Green grasshoppers hid in the grass.

Caterpillars stretched themselves along branches and laid very still. You could not tell them from the limbs of the tree.

Butterflies alighted on trees, closing their wings. There was no way to tell which was the bark, which the leaves, and which the butterflies.

Only tiny Bombardier Beetle crawled along the ground and did not hide.

Puppy chased after him. He wanted to grab him, but Bombardier Beetle stopped short and fired a quick sharp stream at the pup. It went right up his nose!

Puppy yelped and turned around; tail between his legs, he ran, over the meadow and under the gate.

He hid in the kennel and was afraid even to poke his nose out the door for a long, long time.

But the beasts and the birds and the insects once again went about their business, each in his own way.

www.ingramcontent.com/pod-product-compliance
Lightning Source LLC
Chambersburg PA
CBHW081407130726
47998CB00011B/3106